Five reasons why you'll fall in love with Nixie!

 Bumblebees' bottoms! Nixie's always getting in trouble!

A completely new kind of fairy in Fairyland.

Rainbow Fairies meets Horrid Henry!

Full of magical mishaps and ingenious inventions!

 A wonderfully funny story, packed with gorgeous illustrations.

We love Nixie!

'Nixie is a fairy with attitude.'
Waterstones reviewer

'Children who love books about mischievous characters will love this—perfect for Horrid Henry or Angela Nicely fans.'
Amazon reviewer

'Nixie is the coolest fairy ever, although I would not like to have her wand.'
Caitlin

'I really like Nixie because she gets into lots of trouble, which makes me laugh.'
Darcey

Nip's winter magic!

Winter is a busy season for Nip the Winter Fairy. It's up to Nip and the other winter fairies to turn the fairy realm into a magical winter wonderland.

Here's his checklist of really important jobs:

- ☑ SCATTER FROST PATTERNS ON WINDOWS.

- ☑ DECORATE THE TREES AND FAIRY HOUSES WITH ICICLES.

- ☑ FREEZE THE POLISHED PEBBLE POND SO THAT THE FAIRIES CAN SKATE!

- ☑ CREATE SNOW—A LOT OF IT! FAIRYLAND MUST BE COMPLETELY COVERED.

For Tasha,
a Wish Fairy who made her
dream come true, with lots of love

OXFORD
UNIVERSITY PRESS

Great Clarendon Street, Oxford OX2 6DP

Oxford University Press is a department of the University of Oxford.
It furthers the University's objective of excellence in research, scholarship,
and education by publishing worldwide. Oxford is a registered trade mark of
Oxford University Press in the UK and in certain other countries

Copyright © Cas Lester 2015
Illustrations copyright © Ali Pye 2015

The moral rights of the author have been asserted
Database right Oxford University Press (maker)

First published 2015

Data available

ISBN: 978-0-19-274323-7

1 3 5 7 9 10 8 6 4 2

Printed in Great Britain

Paper used in the production of this book is a natural,
recyclable product made from wood grown in sustainable forests.
The manufacturing process conforms to the environmental
regulations of the country of origin.

Nixie
WONKY WINTER WONDERLAND

CAS LESTER

ILLUSTRATED BY ALI PYE

OXFORD
UNIVERSITY PRESS

Contents

Chapter 1
SNOW!

★ ★ ★

'SNOW!' whooped Nixie the Bad, Bad Fairy excitedly, looking through her wonky little window at the most enormous white snowflakes tumbling down outside.

She was still in bed, so she threw off her quilt and leapt up, her little black wings buzzing eagerly against her torn and tatty red fairy dress.

'Yippee! The Winter Fairies have been!' she cried, and her green eyes glittered with glee as she flitted a double back somersault!

At this time of year the Winter Fairies magically scatter **frost** on the windows of the fairy houses, hang **icicles** in the trees, put **ice** on the Polished Pebble Pond, and cover everything with a thick blanket of fresh, white **snow**. Fairyland becomes a beautiful winter wonderland. But for Nixie, it's a wonderful winter . . . playground!

'YA-HOOOOO!!!' she yelled,

'SLEDGING ... SKATING ... AND SNOWBALL FIGHTS!'

Hurriedly clambering into her big red clompy boots, Nixie grabbed her scarf and mittens and crammed her woolly hat onto her black spiky hair.

Then she shoved her wonky black wand into her left boot, so hastily that the red star on the end wobbled about madly, and stuffed her trusty spanner into the other boot. Flinging open her shabby wooden front door, she charged outside.

'WA-HOOO!' she hooted, stamping and stomping deep footprints into the snow. Crisp and crunchy underfoot, but soft and fluffy underneath, it was perfect for snowballs. She scooped up a handful of it, squidged it together, and hurled it as far and as hard as she could.

Wheeee . . .

The snowball sailed all the way to the tree!

Nixie was a good thrower, and a brilliant shot.

Scraping up another handful of snow she patted it into a ball.

Could she hit her wonky wooden front door from the end of her garden path?

Wheeee . . .

12

Yes!

Could she get one on the roof of her little cooking apple house?

Wheeee . . .

Yes!

But could she knock the snow off the apple stalk chimney? She closed one eye, frowned in concentration, then took aim, flung back her arm . . . and

Wheeee . . .

SPLAT!

BUZZZZ!

'Bumblebees' bottoms!' gasped Nixie.

She'd hit Buzby!

The Fairy Godmother's little honeybee assistant was flying overhead on his way to work. The snowball tumbled him over in mid air. He was so surprised he dropped his LilyPad tablet in the snow.

Tut-tutting crossly, he flew down to pick it up.

'Sorry!' cried Nixie, rushing up to help brush the snow off his little furry body.

Buzby waggled his antennae at her irritably, shook himself briskly, and then buzzed off angrily to the Fairy Godmother's house.

'Sorry!' Nixie yelled after him. 'I didn't mean to do it!'

But Buzby had gone.

'Well, even if it was an accident, it was a great shot!' giggled Nixie naughtily.

She decided she'd had enough target practice, so she flitted a front flip and darted up into the clear blue winter sky to find her friends and have some winter wonderland fairy fun . . . starting with a **SNOWBALL BATTLE!**

Chapter 2
WONKY WAND

★ ★ ★

Nixie found Twist the Cobweb Fairy and Fizz the Wish Fairy, busy decorating the outside of the Fairy Grotto. The Fairy Godmother had invited all the fairies to a Midwinter Midnight Feast, so everyone was happily helping with the preparations. Well,

everyone except Nixie, who always thought having fun was much more important than doing chores.

Snow covered the roof of the little wooden cabin like icing on a cake. The windows were painted in peppermint candy stripes, and a green bow hung on the bright red front door.

'It looks like a gingerbread house!' cried Nixie. 'I wish it was—then it would be all crunchy and gingery, and the windows would be minty!'

She darted down and immediately challenged her friends to a snowball fight.

'I'll just finish this!' laughed Fizz, who

was sitting on the chimney, sprinkling the roof with glitter from his magic wand. **TINGLE-TING!**

Nixie groaned impatiently and pulled a face. 'Oh, hurry up!'

'We won't be long!' said Twist, carefully pointing her wand over the door. **TING-A-LING!** A string of pretty icicles streamed out.

'You never put any icicles on my house!' sniffed Nixie huffily.

Twist giggled. 'Don't be daft! There isn't anywhere to hang them on your cooking apple house!'

Nixie grinned and flitted over to the window to peer in at the Fairy Grotto, pressing her nose against the cold glass. Inside it looked snug and cosy with pretty paper **snowflakes** pinned

around the walls and coloured **fairy lanterns** hanging from the ceiling. The tables had already been set out with red and green tablecloths, speckled with **silver stars** and decorated with ivy. Nixie sighed longingly—she couldn't wait for the Midnight Feast!

Fizz called down to her. 'Have you seen Fidget? She's meant to be painting snowflake patterns on the windows.'

'No, I haven't. But I can do it!' cried Nixie, eagerly pulling her tatty red and black wand out of her boot.

'Um . . . is that a good idea?' asked Fizz anxiously. 'I mean, remember when you were meant to be picking crab apples and you turned them into sugar-coated apple doughnuts!'

'Yes! They were scrummy!' laughed Nixie mischievously. 'And it's not my fault my wand's a bit wobbly and doesn't work properly,' she added with a frown, waggling it so that the red star bobbed about crazily.

The fact that Nixie's wand is wonky isn't the only problem. It's also that her wand is as naughty as she is and doesn't always do what she wants it to!

'And what about when you filled the Polished Pebble Pond with bubble bath?' Twist reminded her.

'I didn't mean to do that either!

22

But it was fantastically frothy fun!' giggled Nixie.

'And how about when Adorabella's magic wand suddenly became a wriggly worm—while she was using it!' snorted Fizz.

'Oh, I did that on purpose!' announced Nixie proudly, her green eyes glittering wickedly.

They all burst out laughing. To be fair, Adorabella the Goody-goody Fairy had deserved it. She'd told the Fairy Godmother that Nixie had deliberately poured fairy dust down the Wishing Well, when in actual fact she'd dropped it in herself. The Wishing Well had erupted like a fountain and Nixie hadn't been allowed any magic wishes for a month.

'Anyhow, painting snowflake patterns can't be that hard!' scoffed Nixie as she aimed her wonky wand at the window while Twist and Fizz exchanged worried looks.

ZAPP!

WHOOOOOSH!

To Nixie's horror, three enormous snowballs suddenly burst out of her

wand, headed straight for the window—
and walloped onto the glass with
a **SPLAT!**

The fairies gasped!

'Stupid wand!' wailed Nixie, shaking it
crossly. 'You did that on purpose!'

26

Chapter 3

BRILLIANT SNOWBALL BATTLE

★ ★ ★

Nixie rushed over to the window. Fortunately it wasn't broken—just completely plastered in soft, sticky snow. **PHEW!** Then, grinning wickedly, she scooped up a large fistful, crushed it into a ball, and hurled it up at Fizz on the chimney.

SPLODGE!

She got him right on the knee!

'I'll get you for that!' he laughed. Grabbing a handful of snow from the roof, he scrunched it up and flung it at her, but she darted out of the way and Fizz's snowball whizzed past her and splattered into Twist instead!

'Hey!' she cried, brushing the snow off her woolly hat.

'Sorry!' exclaimed Fizz. 'I was aiming at Nixie!'

Nixie snorted with laughter and stuck her tongue out at both of them! 'Na na na-na nah!' she chanted. 'Can't get me-eee!' And she flitted up in a flash

28

of black and red into the cold bright blue sky.

So then both Fizz and Twist began pelting Nixie with snowballs. *At last*, she thought, her green eyes glinting gleefully, *a snowball battle!*

Wheeee . . .

Twist lobbed a huge great snowball straight at Nixie's face, but Nixie ducked and it soared over her head.

'Missed!' she gloated, promptly snatching up some snow and hurling one right back. Twist squealed and tried to catch it, but the snowball burst in her hands and showered her with snowflakes!

Nixie hooted with laughter, but then Fizz chucked two snowballs at her, one right after another. She swerved and the first one missed, but the second one splattered into her boot, and a cold wet chunk of it slithered down inside to her toes.

'Oooooh! That's cold!' she squealed.

'Gotcha!' hooted Fizz triumphantly from the roof, and then shot behind the chimney so Nixie couldn't get him back.

It was two against one and Nixie couldn't make snowballs fast enough to keep up! She was going to have to do something about that—and she knew exactly what!

'Hang on a minute!' she called, nipping

into the Fairy Grotto. A few minutes later she came out again—armed with a snowball maker made out of a small acorn cup and a wooden spoon, wound together tightly with a piece of ivy!

NIXIE'S MARVELLOUS SNOWBALL MAKER

YOU WILL NEED:

① IVY

② ACORN CUP

③ SPOON

TA DA!!!

It was a genius invention—a cross between an ice cream scoop and a ball thrower. Not only did it speedily roll up dollops of snow into perfect snowballs, but Nixie could also use it to hurl them super fast—and bang on target!

'You'll never beat me now!' she exclaimed.

It was a fierce and furious snowball fight! They completely lost count of who'd hit who, and how many times. Did they care? Nope! At the end of the battle they were covered in snow and breathless from laughing so much.

Darting down to the ground, they

34

brushed each other off and shook the snow from their wings.

'We'd better get on with the decorations,' said Twist. 'Otherwise the Fairy Grotto won't be ready for tonight.'

'What are you doing to help prepare for the Midnight Feast, Nixie?' asked Fizz as he flitted back up to the roof to scatter more glitter round the chimney.

NIXIE GASPED. She should have been fetching holly berries for the Fairy Godmother, to make garlands for the Fairy Grotto, and she'd completely forgotten!

'**Bumblebees' bottoms!**' she groaned. 'I am going to be in so much trouble!' And she zipped home to get her sledge to collect the berries in.

Chapter 4

ADORABELLA, THE GIANT SNOWBALL

★ ★ ★

One of the most fun places in Fairyland is the grassy slope near the Fairy Glade. In the spring the fairies fly blossom kites there, and they play roly-poly down it in the summer, and race rolling conkers in the autumn. But it's best of all in the winter—because it's absolutely perfect for sledging. And so that morning the Winter Fairies had given it an extra double-thick layer of snow and now it looked a huge fluffy white marshmallow!

Adorabella had already finished her task for the Midwinter Midnight Feast. She'd made all her **pretty paper snowflakes** days ago so, bright and early that morning she'd popped into the Fairy Grotto and pinned them all around the walls. And then she'd laid all the tables ready for the feast—without even being asked. The Fairy Godmother was delighted and said Adorabella could spend the rest of the day playing.

She'd headed off to the snowy slope before anybody else, so that she could have all that pure white snow to herself. She was busy making a very tall snowman. It looked a lot like the Fairy Queen, but she was struggling to do the wings. Bits kept dropping off them. So, looking around sneakily to make sure no one was around, she cheated!

TINKLE! TING! Yellow fairy dust, the exact same colour as her frilly fairy dress, streamed from her wand, adding a pair of beautiful snowy wings. Adorabella knew that fairies weren't supposed to waste magic like this, but nobody saw her, and she wanted everyone to think she'd

done it all by herself.

Meanwhile, Nixie was heading to the holly bushes in the Fairy Glade with her wooden sledge. She'd built it herself last winter, adding a sturdy rope made out of cobweb thread and a hook for a lantern so she could sledge in the dark. It wasn't the best sledge in Fairyland— but it was fast!

'Why do I have fetch berries? I mean, what's the point of snow if you can't play in it?' she moaned, her big red boots crunching deep snowy footprints as she stomped. 'And anyhow, there's plenty of time to get berries. Why can't I go sledging?' And then her little face lit

up and slowly broke into a cheeky grin.

'In fact, I probably should go sledging in case the snow starts melting. It'd be a shame to waste it.'

So she headed off to the snowy slope, plonked her sledge down at the top, and jumped on. She was just about to kick off when she saw Adorabella, slap bang in the middle of the slope below her, making a silly, stupid snowman!

'Hey, *Adora-smella*!' yelled Nixie rudely. **'Get out of the way!'**

'No! Why should I?' shouted back Adorabella haughtily.

'Because I'm sledging!'

'Go somewhere else!'

'There isn't anywhere else! We always sledge here!' bellowed Nixie crossly.

'I don't care!' gloated Adorabella. 'I was here first. And anyway, you won't get very far on that wonky old sledge!'

'**MOVE!**' bawled Nixie. Her little black wings buzzed angrily and her face went redder than her dress.

'Can't make me,' pouted Adorabella, folding her arms and glaring challengingly at Nixie.

OH, YES, I CAN! thought Nixie impishly. *Then you'll see what this wonky old sledge can do!* And she stuck out her legs, in their black holey tights, and kicked off hard, with her big boots.

Nixie's sledge started sliding downhill, very quickly picking up speed.

'YAHOO! This is BRILLIANT!' she hollered.

WHOOOOSH!

She hurtled down towards Adorabella and her silly, stupid snowman, expecting her to jump out of the way. But Adorabella just stood there smugly, with her arms folded and, as soon as Nixie got near, Adorabella flicked her wand and TING-a-TING! WHOOSH! A stream of fairy dust splattered onto Nixie's sledge, stopping it so suddenly that Nixie was hurled right out.

SCRUNCH!

'Serves you right!' gloated Adorabella as Nixie struggled up, furiously shaking snow off her wings.

Nixie's green eyes glittered angrily. 'I'll get you back for that!' she cried, snatching her wonky wand out of her boot and pointing at Adorabella's snowman, intending to knock it flat!

'**Nooooo!**' wailed Adorabella, jumping in front of it to protect it.

ZAP! FIZZZ!

Purple sparks shot out of Nixie's wand and knocked Adorabella clean off her feet. She landed flat on her back and

promptly started rolling down the slope, gathering snow as she did so.

'**HELP!**' screeched Adorabella, spinning round and round, and picking up so much snow that by the time she got to the bottom she looked like a giant snowball with just her head and legs sticking out!

Nixie jumped back on her sledge and swished down to her, laughing her head off.

'I'm telling the Fairy Godmother on you!' howled Adorabella as she struggled to her feet and waddled off furiously to the Fairy Godmother's house, in a big snowy huff.

'Bumblebees' bottoms!' groaned Nixie. 'Now I'm in trouble, again!'

Chapter 5
A FEROCIOUS BLIZZARD

★ ★ ★

Nixie turned to climb back up, dragging her sledge behind her for another go, but saw, to her fury, that Adorabella had ruined the slope! Not only had she used loads of snow to build her silly, stupid snowman, but she'd taken tons more away with her, all

rolled up in her giant snowball coat!

'Typical!' snorted Nixie angrily. 'How am I supposed to go sledging on that?'

Just then the Winter Fairies flew by overhead and waved cheerfully at Nixie. They were on their way to check that the ice on the Polished Pebble Pond was thick enough to skate on safely.

Nixie called out to the nearest one. 'Nip! I need you!'

Nip darted down to join her. 'What's up, Nixie?' he asked brightly.

'Look what Adorabella did to the slope!' complained Nixie bitterly. 'It's all messed up. It needs more snow—and lots of it!'

Nip laughed. He was always more than happy to make snow! 'Stand back then,' he said and raised his white wand.

TING! Whooooosh!

A stream of huge fluffy snowflakes poured out and onto the slope.

'Can I have a go?' asked Nixie.

Nip grinned at her. 'Well, only if you promise not to plaster everything with whipped cream, or icing sugar, or . . . mashed potato!' he teased. 'You know what you're like!'

'It's not me, it's my tatty old wand!' retorted Nixie indignantly. 'And anyway, I've already made snow today,' she boasted casually. (Of course, she didn't admit that she'd nearly broken a window of the Fairy Grotto when she did so!)

'All right then, but be careful!' warned Nip.

Nixie confidently pulled her wand out

50

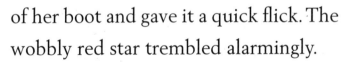

of her boot and gave it a quick flick. The wobbly red star trembled alarmingly.

ZAAPPP!

PHUTT!

FIZZLE!

Nothing happened! Not even a single tiny snowflake squeezed out.

'Stupid, wonky old wand!' moaned Nixie in frustration, and shook it roughly. The red star wobbled so hard it looked like it might drop off.

'Steady!' cried Nip anxiously.

Nixie's little black wings buzzed with

concentration. She twirled her wand again, and tried to not let the star wobble so much.

ZAP! Fizzle . . .

A thin trickle of tiny snowflakes dribbled out.

'Yahoo!' she gloated and did it again.

ZAP! Swoooooosh!

This time a good dollop of fluffy snow spluttered out!

'Told you!' she bragged, her green eyes glittering with glee.

'Come on then!' called Nip, flitting up and aiming his wand again.

TING! Whoooooosh!

ZAP! Swoooooosh!

The two fairies zipped around, covering the slope with layers and layers of crisp fresh snow.

But after a while, after quite a short while in fact, Nixie got bored.

'It's very slow,' she complained.

'You can't rush snow,' grinned Nip.

'I bet I can,' muttered Nixie. She shook her wand violently and whirled it round rapidly. The red star wobbled furiously and …

ZAAPPP! **VEROOOOM …**

ZHWOOOOOM …

a ferocious blizzard gushed out! And to Nixie's horror, Nip was instantly swept up in it and then dumped in a snowdrift!

'Oh, no!' she gasped, rushing to help him. She threw down her wand and scrabbled to dig him out of the snow with her hands.

'Don't worry. I'm fine,' he said, clambering out and shaking himself free of snow. But the blizzard was still pouring out of Nixie's wand.

VEROOOM . . .

SCHWOOOSH!

Huge piles of snow built up all around. **'Make it STOP!'** begged Nip.

Bravely, Nixie flew into the swirling blizzard, and snatched up her wand.

'Stop!' she ordered, **'STOP!'**

But it wouldn't. She tried shoving it upside down into the snow, but the mound of snow just got bigger and bigger.

'What are we going to do?' wailed Nip.

There was only one thing to do.

Desperately, they dashed off to the Fairy Godmother.

56

Chapter 6

SNOWSTORM iN THE KiTCHEN

Tabitha Quicksilver, the Fairy Godmother, loved winter and especially the Midwinter Midnight Feast. It was her favourite party in the whole fairy year.

She'd spent the morning making enchanted snow dome shakers for

everyone. Buzby picked one up and shook it gently. The little scene inside **glowed with magic** while pearly white glitter tumbled down like snow on to a tiny little fir tree.

Then she'd made lots of pretty bead snowflakes and hung them on ribbons in the windows.

'Fairyland looks so lovely in the snow,' she had sighed to Buzby, gazing blissfully at the winter wonderland outside.

Today, her little pumpkin house looked breathtakingly pretty. Its rounded dark orange walls were sprinkled with snow. The golden glow of the lights inside spilled through the little round windows and tinted the snow pale yellow. A wisp of smoke curled up from the chimney, white against the clear blue winter sky.

Buzby was less keen on winter—what with getting hit by Nixie's snowball and then dropping his LilyPad in the snow. But he had soon cheered up in the warmth of the kitchen, and fortunately his tablet wasn't broken. He'd used it to look up making paper chains on the

FairyNet and was now happily sticking shiny paper hoops together.

The Fairy Godmother had just picked up her large scissors to start cutting paper lanterns when Adorabella **burst** into her kitchen looking like a giant snowball! Fairy Godmothers aren't easily flustered, and so Tabitha Quicksilver hadn't even batted an eyelid. She'd just calmly flicked her wand and made the snow disappear with a **sprinkle of silvery fairy dust**, settled Adorabella in a chair, and made her a large, soothing mug of hot chocolate.

Now Adorabella was sitting finishing her drink, feeling cosy and dry. But

her snowball disaster had left her with messy hair, a crumpled fairy dress, and a very bad temper. She was brooding on how to get her own back on Nixie and land her in trouble.

'It was all Nixie's fault,' she reminded the Fairy Godmother, her bottom lip trembling.

'I haven't got time to deal with Nixie right now,' replied Tabitha Quicksilver impatiently.

'AREN'T YOU GOING TO PUNISH HER?' sulked Adorabella.

'Not right now, no,' announced the Fairy Godmother, hurriedly cutting out paper lanterns.

'BUT AREN'T YOU EVEN GOING TO TELL HER OFF?' wailed Adorabella indignantly.

Tabitha Quicksilver raised one eyebrow and shot her a look.

'THAT'S NOT FAIRY FAIR!' whined Adorabella.

'It's as fair as a Fairy Godmother can make it!' snapped Tabitha Quicksilver sharply. 'I'm very busy today! Fidget promised to help me make the paper lanterns but I haven't seen her all day, and I haven't even started on the garlands for the Fairy Grotto because Nixie hasn't brought me any holly berries!'

Buzby tut-tutted sympathetically and his wings buzzed busily.

'Nixie's so lazy,' gloated Adorabella smugly. 'You can't rely on her to do anything, can you?' she added, smiling innocently at the Fairy Godmother.

Tabitha Quicksilver didn't answer so Adorabella continued. 'I know I've done all my chores already, but I don't mind helping you—indoors,' she added quickly. She was just putting her mug down when . . .

SLAM!

The door flew open, and Nixie and Nip burst into the kitchen—bringing Nixie's wand and the blizzard in with them!

Chapter 7

ADORABELLA, THE SNOWMAN

✦ ✦ ✦

Whooosh! Icy cold snow spurted out of Nixie's wand, plastering the entire kitchen, and splattering the Fairy Godmother and Adorabella, who both shrieked with shock. Buzby grabbed his LilyPad and darted under the table for safety.

His paper chains, piled on top of the table, disappeared under a snowdrift, along with the scissors, the glue, the paper lanterns, and the snow dome shakers.

'It won't stop!' yelled Nixie, shaking her wobbly wand and managing to accidentally-on-purpose point it in Adorabella's direction. She grinned wickedly as snow covered Adorabella from head to foot until she looked like a snowman!

Adorabella **SCREAMED**, Nip gasped in horror, and Nixie giggled naughtily.

At times of crisis there is nothing more useful than a Fairy Godmother.

Casually, Tabitha Quicksilver picked up her wand and—**TING! WHOOOSH!**— a cascade of purple stars showered onto Nixie's wand. It shuddered, gave a couple of snowy sneezes, and the blizzard stopped immediately.

With great self-control the Fairy Godmother turned to Nixie and said, 'I do wish you'd left your wand outside, dear.'

'**Ooops!**' said Nixie, eyeing the snow-filled kitchen with dismay.

To be fair, Nixie hadn't dared leave her wand outside and risk losing it. She'd lost it once before and there had been no end of trouble.

But perhaps she should have left it outside on this occasion. She definitely hadn't meant to cover the Fairy Godmother's kitchen in snow, even if she had meant to ever-so-slightly smother Adorabella!

'I'M FROZEN!' screeched Adorabella dramatically.

Tabitha Quicksilver raised her wand again.

TING-a-TING!

The indoor snowdrift instantly turned into a huge heap of frothy bubbles, which floated up and burst harmlessly so that soon there was absolutely no sign of the wintry chaos that had completely filled

the kitchen only a few moments earlier.

POP-POPPATY-POP!

Nip sighed with relief and Buzby clambered back out from under the table.

But Adorabella was fuming!

'You did that on purpose!' she screamed at Nixie.

'No, I didn't!'

'Did!'

'Didn't!'

'You big fat hairy-fairy fibber!' shrieked Adorabella.

'Fairies! FAIRIES! How is this helping?' cried the Fairy Godmother.

Buzby waggled his antennae disapprovingly.

Adorabella and Nixie stood glaring at each other with their arms crossed.

Nip was the only fairy to say 'sorry' to the Fairy Godmother.

'Thank you, Nip, but it wasn't your fault,' she said to him kindly and then, glancing at the clock, she told him to run along since she was sure he still had lots to do, and even if he didn't, she did! Gratefully, Nip fluttered off to find the other Winter Fairies.

Tabitha Quicksilver turned to Nixie. 'Whatever am I going to do with you?' she asked in despair.

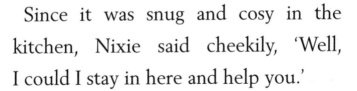

Since it was snug and cosy in the kitchen, Nixie said cheekily, 'Well, I could I stay in here and help you.'

'No, you can't!' snapped Adorabella.

'It's not up to you!' retorted Nixie hotly.

Tabitha Quicksilver took a deep breath and reminded herself that Fairy Godmothers aren't supposed to lose their tempers.

'FAIRIES!' she scolded. 'I'll decide who gets to help me and who doesn't!'

'But that's not fairy fair! I asked first!' wailed Adorabella. 'And anyhow,' she added slyly, 'Nixie hasn't even got the holly berries for you yet!'

'YOU BIG FAT HAIRY-FAIRY TROUBLEMAKER!'

blurted Nixie, and stuck her tongue out at Adorabella.

'Nixie!' tutted the Fairy Godmother.

Behind her back, Adorabella smirked at Nixie and two pretty little dimples appeared in her cheeks.

'Honestly, Nixie, I can't trust you to do anything, can I?' sighed Tabitha Quicksilver. Then she added, 'I think Buzby had better get the holly berries.'

Nixie's little black wings drooped sadly—and so did Buzby's! It was very cold for a honeybee outside.

'At least I know you'll get job done,'

added the Fairy Godmother, smiling at
her assistant.

Buzby's little stripy body instantly puffed up with pride and he immediately fluttered out importantly, in search of holly.

'And you,' said Tabitha Quicksilver to Nixie, 'can go and find Fidget. I can't think where she's got to.'

'Fine!' sighed Nixie glumly, shooting Adorabella one last angry look, before stomping out of the door, slamming it behind her.

Chapter 8

SNOWED IN!

Flying high above Fairyland, Nixie looked down longingly at all the snow. She'd hardly got to play in it at all today.

She darted over to the Polished Pebble Pond, looking for Fidget. The Winter Fairies had put a good thick layer of ice on top, and now lots of fairies were skating on it. Twist and Fizz were trying to do a figure of eight, and Nip and the other Winter Fairies were having races, but Fidget wasn't with them and they said they hadn't seen her at all.

Flying over the Fairy Dell, Nixie could see Dulcie the Tooth Fairy and Willow the Tree Fairy having a terrific snowball fight. She fluttered down, wishing she could join in, but knowing she had to find her friend first.

They hadn't seen Fidget either.

'Maybe she's stayed at home?' suggested Dulcie.

'What, and miss all the fun in the

snow?' asked Willow doubtfully.

It didn't seem likely, but Nixie fluttered off to Fidget's house to see if she was there.

The sun was beginning to go down as she neared Fidget's home, and it was starting to get dark. Nixie looked all about her but she couldn't see Fidget's house.

Where is it? she wondered. Round and round in circles she flew and then went lower and lower, but she still couldn't see it. *This is silly! How can a house disappear?* she thought. *I can't see anything but snow!*

'BUMBLEBEES' BOTTOMS!'

she gasped. 'That's it! I can't see Fidget's house because of all the snow!'

She fluttered down to where she thought the house ought to be, and sure enough there it was, almost hidden in a snowdrift.

A blanket of snow covered the roof, most of the windows, and the front door. Nixie couldn't even find the door to knock on it, so she called out loudly. 'Fidget? FIDGET! Are you in there?'

'Nixie, is that you?' replied Fidget with relief. Her voice sounded as though it was coming from just under the roof!

Looking up, Nixie could see Fidget's

face in the little round attic window. Fidget waved at her and Nixie fluttered up.

'I can't get out!' called Fidget through the glass. 'I've been stuck in all day!

I don't want to be trapped here all night and miss the Midnight Feast!' she added forlornly. 'Can you go and get the Fairy Godmother?'

But Nixie didn't want to bother the Fairy Godmother. She was determined to prove that she could be trusted to do something right today!

So she asked Fidget sensibly, 'Can't you get out of the attic window?'

'No,' replied Fidget gloomily. 'It doesn't open!'

'Don't worry,' exclaimed Nixie brightly. 'I'll think of something.'

'Why can't you just go and get the Fairy Godmother?' asked Fidget.

'Because she's very busy,' replied Nixie. 'And anyway,' she announced confidently, 'there's no need. I'll soon get you out!'

'But how?' asked Fidget anxiously, hoping that Nixie wouldn't try to use her wonky wand with the usual disastrous results.

To be honest, just at that moment, Nixie wasn't too sure what she was going to do.

Chapter 9

BiTS AND BOBS AND ODDS AND ENDS

✦ ✦ ✦

Nixie always believes the best thing to do about a problem is to look at it carefully, then have a good think, and come up with a practical way to solve it. So she fluttered down to look at the heap of snow blocking Fidget's front door.

It was much too deep for her to clear with her hands—or even with a shovel—and she didn't dare use magic, not after the accident at the Fairy Grotto with the snowballs and the blizzard in the Fairy Godmother's kitchen! So she kept her tatty wand safely in her boot and thought hard.

'Fidget!' she called suddenly. 'I've had a brilliant idea.'

Uh oh, thought Fidget and her heart sank. Nixie's 'brilliant' ideas often caused more chaos and catastrophe than her deliberately naughty ones!

'I just need to go and get something. Wait here and I'll be back before you

can say "wonky wands",' promised Nixie confidently.

'Oh, all right,' called Fidget miserably, thinking how much simpler it would be if Nixie would just fetch the Fairy Godmother instead!

Nixie darted off to collect her sledge from the snowy slope where she'd left it, and then she hurried home to her workshop.

Nixie's workshop is a little wooden shed leaning against one side of her cooking apple house. A large lantern hangs from the ceiling, making it bright and cheery, and a heater keeps it cosy and warm— even in the middle of winter.

All along one wall Nixie's tools hang neatly on hooks (except for her trusty spanner, which she always keeps tucked in her right boot). There's a hammer, a pair of pliers, and two saws, and in the corner she keeps a broom, a large shovel, and a garden rake.

In the middle of the workshop is a long wooden bench with tubs and boxes crammed underneath, full of all sorts of **bits and bobs** that might be useful for making or mending things. There are acorn cups, conker cases, large seeds, bits of twig, and a reel of spider's web plus lots of **odds and ends** that other fairies have thrown away.

Nixie rootled about and dug out an old metal tray.

'Perfect!' she announced and, picking up her hammer and some nails, set about fixing it onto the front of her sledge.

BASH! BANG! THUMP!

Deftly, she knocked in the nails with a few satisfying wallops from her hammer.

'That'll do the job!' she said proudly.

Nixie had turned her sledge into a snowplough!

Quickly, she threw in her large shovel, hooked on the lamp, because it was really dark by now, and raced back to rescue her friend.

It wasn't very long before Fidget heard Nixie calling, 'I'm back! I'll soon get you out,' and, looking out of her attic window, she saw the warm glow of a light crossing the dark snowy night, and Nixie whizzing up on her sledge.

Nixie got straight on with the job. She dragged her snowplough sledge to the front of Fidget's house, then got behind it and shoved with all her fairy might. SCRUNCH! SHOVE!

Slowly but surely, Nixie forced the

snowplough through the snowdrift. The metal tray on the front pushed the snow to the sides of the path. It took several goes, and Nixie was soon hot and panting, but finally she managed to clear the way to the front door. Then, grabbing her shovel, she dug out the last of the snow and Fidget was freed.

'**WOOHOO!**' yelled Nixie triumphantly, flitting a gleeful back flip.

'Thank you!' cried Fidget, rushing out and hugging her.

Then Fidget grabbed her woolly hat and warm scarf, and they both darted off to find their friends and join in the fun before the Midnight Feast.

Chapter 10

ADORABELLA BOSSY BRITCHES

★ ★ ★

It was very late. Stars twinkled in the dark sky and the ice on the Polished Pebble Pond sparkled in the moonlight as the fairies whizzed around on their skates, squealing and clutching onto each other to stop themselves slipping over. Their eyes shone and their cheeks

glowed and you could see their breath in the cold night air.

Twist and Fidget were holding hands and trying to do a spin, but suddenly, **WHOOOPS!** Fidget's skates shot from under her and **BUMP!** she landed on her bottom, pulling Twist down on top of her! They burst out laughing.

Adorabella hated falling over, so she skated slowly and daintily round the edge. Swerving carefully to avoid Twist and Fidget, who were struggling to stand up, she instantly collided with Nixie who was racing past her. Adorabella lost her balance, screamed, and tumbled over backwards, and

Nixie roared with laughter.

'You did that deliberately!' wailed Adorabella. Nixie grinned wickedly.

Nixie isn't a brilliant skater, not like Nip and the other Winter Fairies who can do difficult jumps and double spins and triple twists, but she is fearless—and fast!

'YA-HOOOOO!' she yelled, speeding along and overtaking everyone. But then Nip overtook her—and he was going backwards!

Nixie instantly spun round and tried to copy him. But skating backwards was a lot trickier than she realized, mainly because she couldn't see where she was going—and she blundered straight into Fizz.

'Watch out!' he laughed.

'Ooops! Sorry!' squeaked Nixie, clutching hold of him and making him wobble. Fizz instantly flung out his arm to grab Twist, but she was holding onto Fidget and so they all walloped onto the ice in a muddled heap!

'Mind out!' and 'Help!' squealed the other fairies as SKIDDLE-SKID, SLIDE, BUMP, and WHOOOOPS! one by one they all tumbled into a huge pile-up in the middle of the frozen pond!

All except Adorabella, who was going so slowly that she was able to stop in time, tut-tutting smugly.

Slipping and sliding, and helpless

with laughter, the fairies scrabbled and struggled to stand, and finally managed to help each other up.

'Everybody has to be more careful, and go the same way!' bossed Adorabella, skating off clockwise round the pond, and ordering everyone to follow her.

It worked for a while, with all the fairies gliding steadily round in the same direction, until Nixie got stuck behind Adorabella, who was going about as fast as a sleepy slug!

'Move over, frilly knickers!' she yelled crossly.

'No, why should I?' cried Adorabella.

'Because you're much too slow!' complained Nixie, trying to skate past her. 'You're holding everybody up!'

'No overtaking!' howled Adorabella, grabbing at her.

'Says who?' snapped Nixie rudely, giving Adorabella a crafty shove so that she did an almighty wobble and nearly fell over again.

'Right, that does it! As soon as we get to the Fairy Grotto I'm telling the Fairy Godmother!' screeched Adorabella.

Nixie stuck her tongue out, and sped up to catch up with Nip.

'This is boring,' moaned Nip. 'Why do

we have to do what bossy old Adorabella says?'

'We don't!' replied Nixie. 'Let's play tag! You're "It"!' she grinned, punching him playfully and whizzing off across the ice.

'Hey! Not fair!' laughed Nip, hurriedly chasing after her.

Giggling and squealing delightedly, the other fairies ducked and darted out of their way as Nip and Nixie charged crazily in between them. And soon everyone was racing around madly and having fun again.

Everyone except Adorabella. 'You're going the wrong way!' she bawled furiously.

'**Don't care!**' yelled Nixie, whooshing past her.

Nixie looked over her shoulder. Nip was right behind her—he'd almost caught up with her! She squealed and put on a rapid burst of speed, shooting off, without looking where she was going.

'**NIXIE! LOOK OUT!**' cried Fidget.

Nixie turned and gasped in horror! She was heading towards the edge of the pond and hurtling straight for a tree!

'Bumblebees' bottoms! HELP!'
she yelled.

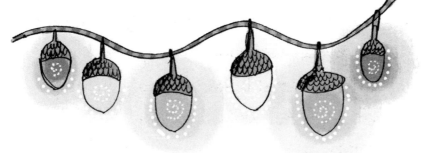

101

102

Chapter 11

MAGICAL MIDWINTER MIDNIGHT FEAST

★ ★ ★

Nixie shot across the ice—she couldn't stop! Suddenly she saw someone skating slowly and daintily across in front of her.

It was Adorabella.

'Mind out!' warned Nixie, waving her arms frantically.

Adorabella desperately tried to scramble out of the way, but Nixie was going much too fast and **CRASH!** Nixie smashed into her at full pelt . . . and Adorabella was sent hurtling off towards the tree instead of Nixie!

'Help!' she screamed.

Her pretty yellow skates hit a tree root hidden in the snowy bank and she was thrown through the air— **WHEEEEE!**—landing upside down in a snowdrift, with her legs waving in the air.

THWUMPFF!

Everyone could see her frilly fairy knickers! Trying hard not to laugh, all

the fairies rushed over to help.

But Nixie got there first and, grabbing Adorabella's waggling upturned legs, pulled with all her fairy might.

It was just at that moment that the Fairy Godmother arrived.

'**NIXIE!**' she cried in horror. 'Whatever are you doing to Adorabella now?'

'Rescuing her,' replied Nixie, and, digging her little fairy feet into the snow, she gave Adorabella a huge heave and—**WHUMPH!**—she pulled her out of the snowdrift.

Poor Adorabella was smothered in freezing cold snow—for the third time that day!

Clenching her fists in fury, she launched herself at Nixie. 'I'll get you back for that!'

'THAT'S ENOUGH!' bellowed Tabitha Quicksilver sternly, stopping Adorabella in her tracks. Then, turning to the other fairies, she calmly asked what happened.

Twist explained that Nixie had accidently knocked Adorabella into a snowdrift and had then rushed over to rescue her.

'And she rescued me too today,' piped up Fidget. 'I was snowed in but she turned her sledge into a snowplough and dug me out of my house.'

'You made a snowplough, Nixie? What a BRILLIANT IDEA!' exclaimed Tabitha Quicksilver, very impressed.

Nixie grinned and tried to look modest. Then, to everyone's delight, the Fairy Godmother announced it was time for the Midwinter Midnight Feast, and **TING-a-TING!** a shower of fairy dust from her wand quickly turned their skates back into ordinary shoes (or big clompy boots, in Nixie's case) and they all darted off excitedly to the Fairy Grotto. Adorabella complained angrily about Nixie to the Fairy Godmother all the way there! Nixie grinned at Fizz and rolled her eyes.

Buzby had hung the snowflake paper lanterns and the holly berry garlands outside the Fairy Grotto, and the Fairy

Godmother had covered the front door with enormous jelly beans. It looked even more like a gingerbread house! Warm golden light spilled invitingly from the windows and onto the snow.

The fairies all trooped inside, their noses running, cheeks zinging, and toes tingling in the warmth. It smelled so wonderfully of chocolate and roasting chestnuts, they could almost taste it!

The Fairy Godmother clapped her hands.

'Hold out your magic wands!' she ordered, raising her own, and TING! suddenly it was snowing indoors—but it was fairy dust and not snowflakes that floated onto their wands. They sparkled and glittered and shone with magic. All except Nixie's—she'd held up her spanner by mistake! And now that was all **sparkly** and **glittery!**

'Noooooo!' she groaned and the other fairies hooted with laughter.

At last it was time to eat! They all tucked in to hot chocolate with mini marshmallows and swirls of whipped cream, ginger icicle biscuits sprinkled with white sugar stars, marzipan fruit cake with snowflake icing, coconut snowballs with white chocolate coating, spiced hot apple fruit cup, and roasted chestnuts . . .

Nixie munched away, warm and toasty by the fire, her little fairy face smudged with a sticky brown hot chocolate moustache. She smiled to herself secretly as she thought about all the wonderful midwinter mischief and mayhem she could get up to tomorrow!

Acknowledgements

Huge thanks to:

Gaia Banks—because 'Life itself
is a wonderful fairy tale' (*Hans Christian
Andersen)*—thank you.

Kathy Webb and **Gill Sore** at OUP—because
'Nothing can be truer than fairy wisdom'
(*Douglas Jerrold)*—except yours.

Ali Pye—because 'Everybody's got a fairyland
of their own' (*P.L. Travers)*—but yours is more
magical than most.

Annie Beth—because you were and still are the
original Bad, Bad Fairy and 'I do believe in fairies!
I do! I do!' (*J.M. Barrie)*

and

My boys—because 'Magic is believing in yourself.
If you can do that, you can make anything
happen.' (*Johann Wolfgang von Goethe)*. And
anyhow, 'It's still magic, even if you know how
it's done.' (*Terry Pratchett)*

A Little Bit About Me . . .

I used to make children's television programmes for CBBC like *Jackanory* and *The Story of Tracy Beaker*. But now I'm writing books for children instead.

This is great because it means I can spend more time with my family, and the chickens, the cats, and Bramble, my daft dog. And I get to do lots of school visits, which I love. I'm also the author of the Harvey Drew books—comedy adventures set in outer space.

I've never had a fairy costume, but I do remember being an angel in the school nativity play. I wore a long white dress and a silver tinsel halo. Unfortunately, I had a

black eye, which spoiled the look a bit.
But my daughter did have a fairy costume.

It was pink and orange and she liked to wear it with wellington boots and a green plastic army hat. I thought it was a great look—and Nixie the Bad, Bad Fairy was born!

This is my favourite picture of me. It was taken by my daughter's friend when she was nine. We call it 'The Cas in the Hat'.

Cas

I have wanted to illustrate books for almost as long as I can remember. When I was little I spent lots of time drawing and thinking up stories. I often got told off for 'having my nose in a book' or doodling when I was supposed to be helping my family—now I have to nag my own children for exactly the same reasons!

It took me a while to achieve my ambition; I studied fashion at Central St Martins and worked as a writer before taking an MA course in illustration at Kingston University. While at Kingston, I was commissioned to illustrate *Where is Fred?* by Edward Hardy.

I have since worked for publishers including Oxford University Press, Campbell Books, Egmont, Nosy Crow, Orchard Books, HarperCollins, and Stripes. I live in Twickenham with my family and two very shy guinea pigs; I feel very lucky to do something that I love for a living.

Best wishes
Ali

Tabitha Quicksilver's Snow-covered Gingerbread Trees

Sweet, gingery, and delicious!

INGREDIENTS LIST

- 75g SOFTENED BUTTER
- 50g CASTER SUGAR
- 1/2 TSP BICARBONATE OF SODA
- 3 TBSP GOLDEN SYRUP
- 2 EGG YOLKS
- 250g PLAIN FLOUR
- 1 TSP GROUND CINNAMON
- 1 TSP GROUND GINGER
- 300g ICING SUGAR

1 Preheat your oven to 180°C, gas mark 4.

3 Then add the bicarbonate of soda, golden syrup, and egg yolks and mix well.

2 Start your dough by beating together the caster sugar and butter with a wooden spoon until the mixture goes smooth.

4 Sift in the flour, cinnamon, and ginger then bring together with a wooden spoon—you should now have a big lump of gingery dough.

5 On a lightly-floured surface knead the dough with your hands until you can feel it become firm and springy. Once kneaded, chill your dough in the fridge for 30 minutes.

6 Take your dough out of the fridge and roll it out with a rolling pin to around 1cm thickness. If you have a tree cutter, press this into the dough to form your trees. But if not, don't worry—you can ask your assistant to help you cut tree shapes into the dough with a knife—a simple triangle shape works well.

7 Next, place your trees onto a lined and greased baking tray and pop into the oven. Bake them for 10–12 minutes.

8 Once baked, cool your trees on a rack.

9 Now it's time to ice your trees! Mix your icing sugar with 3–4 tbsp of water and spread the icing over each tree shape.

Your gingerbread trees are ready and taste great just as they are, but if you'd like to decorate them with sprinkles or sweets, do so!

YOU WILL NEED AN ASSISTANT, SO MAKE SURE THAT AN ADULT HELPS YOU.

Nixie's Swirly Snowstorm in a Bottle

You don't need Nixie's wonky wand to create a blustery blizzard. Try creating a snowstorm in your home, safely kept inside a bottle.

YOU WILL NEED:

- A CLEAR PLASTIC BOTTLE
- WATER
- GLITTER
- WASHING-UP LIQUID
- A PENCIL

WATER

1 Fill your bottle three quarters of the way up with water and a couple of drops of washing up liquid.

2 Next add some sparkly magic with some glitter. **Top Tip:** For an easy way to add glitter, wet a pencil and dip this into your glitter, then dip the pencil into your bottle of water—the glitter should come off the pencil and swirl into the water.

3 Screw the lid onto the bottle as tightly as you can. Ask your assistant to twist the lid too.

4 Once the lid is secure, tip the bottle upside down holding it tightly by the neck. Swirl the bottle around in a circular motion lots of times to generate the snow storm power.

5 Stop and look inside the bottle. You should see a swirling tornado of glitter.

YOU WILL NEED AN ASSISTANT, SO MAKE SURE THAT AN ADULT HELPS YOU.

Nip's Winter Wonderland Lantern

Light up a gloomy winter evening with this frosted lantern.

YOU WILL NEED:
- AN EMPTY GLASS JAR
- A POT
- PVA GLUE
- AN OLD NEWSPAPER
- A SPONGE
- A TEALIGHT
- FOOD COLOURING OR PAINT
- GLITTER

OPTIONAL:
- TISSUE PAPER AND A SMALL PAINT BRUSH

1 Start by preparing your glue. Put some glue into a pot and thin it with a little water. If you'd like to make a coloured lantern, add a few drops of food colouring or paint to the glue and mix well.

FOOD COLOUR

GLUE

2 Place your jar on an old newspaper and using the sponge carefully cover the outside of the jar with a light coating of the glue mix.

3 Add some sparkle by sprinkling glitter over the wet glue.

4 You could also add tissue paper to your lantern. Try cutting the paper into shapes—stars would work well—and then stick them onto the wet glue, pressing them down with a damp paintbrush.

5 Once your lantern is dry, add a tealight, and light up any space with some winter magic.

Get ready for more Nixie mischief in . . .

SPLASHY SUMMER SWIM

POING, POUNCE, SPLAT!

'Bumblebees' bottoms! I can't do it!' groaned Nixie the Bad, Bad Fairy. She'd just landed in a crumpled heap on a cobweb, with her bottom up in the air—for the umpteenth time that morning.

Nixie's friends roared with laughter!

'You nearly did it! grinned Fizz the Wish Fairy.

It was a brilliantly hot summer day and Nixie and her friends were trampolining on a cobweb, seeing how many bottom-sits they could do. Twist the Cobweb Fairy was ahead with fifteen. Fidget the Butterfly Fairy and Fizz had both done eleven.

But Nixie was hopeless! She kept ending up sprawled across the cobweb with her big red clompy boots all tangled up!

'Try again,' cried Fidget.

'You're not bouncing high enough,' called Twist.

Nixie's black wings buzzed with concentration, and her grubby little face screwed up into a frown.

BOUNCE . . . BOING . . .

Her tatty dress flashed bright red in the clear blue sky as she jumped super-high.

'Here goes!' she yelled, but . . .

BOING, BOUNCE, SPLAT!

'Ooof!' she gasped, landing flat on her back with her legs waggling in the air!

Everyone fell about laughing!

'You're meant to stick your legs out when you sit!' hooted Fidget.

'I can't!' exclaimed Nixie, 'Not, in these great big boots!'

'Well, take them off!' suggested Fizz.

But Nixie didn't want to take her boots off. It was where she kept her magic wand.

She was very tempted to use her wonky black wand, with its wobbly red star, right now. Perhaps she could magic her boots and make them lighter! But she couldn't exactly trust her naughty wand to do as it was told.

'I give up!' she grinned and did some really high bounces instead.

POING, POUNCE! POING!

As she bounced she could see Briar the Flower Fairy and Willow the Tree Fairy watering the plants in the Fairy Glade.

POUNCE!

Briar had emptied her watering can already, so Willow was filling it up again from the Twisty Trickle Stream that splashed its way round the Fairy Glade and down to the Polished Pebble Pond. It looked like very hot work.

POING!

On the other side of the Fairy Glade, Nixie saw Adorabella the Goody-goody Fairy lying on a daisy, sunbathing. Her eyes were closed and she was fanning herself with a small leaf.

POUNCE!

Nixie heard Briar call over to Adorabella. 'Can you come and give us a hand?'

But Adorabella just wafted her leaf pathetically and groaned. 'I'm much too hot to do anything!'

POING!

Nixie bounced up again in time to see Willow and Briar roll their eyes at each other, and then carry on with the watering.

Huh typical! thought Nixie, slowing down and bouncing to a standstill. *Why should Adorabella get to lie around doing nothing, while Briar and Willow are doing all the work? In fact, I'm going to have to do something about that!*

A wicked grin stole across her little face, and a look of sheer mischief shot into her glittering green eyes.

'I'm going to help Briar and Willow,' she announced to her friends and, giggling gleefully, she darted up off the trampoline and flew over to the Fairy Path.

Nixie had just had a brilliantly, naughty idea!

Love Nixie? Then we know you're going to enjoy reading about these fantastic characters too . . .